Frankenstein

Retold from the Mary Shelley
original by Deanna McFadden

Illustrated by Jamel Akib

Sterling Publishing Co., Inc.
New York

Library of Congress Cataloging-in-Publication Data

McFadden, Deanna.
  Frankenstein / retold [from] the Mary Shelley original ; abridged by
Deanna McFadden ; illustrated by Jamel Akib.
    p. cm.—(Classic starts)
 Summary: An abridged version of the novel in which a monster assembled
by a scientist from parts of dead bodies develops a mind of his own as he
learns to loathe himself and hate his creator.
  ISBN 1-4027-2666-X
 [1. Monsters—Fiction. 2. Horror stories.] I. Akib, Jamel, ill. II. Shelley, Mary
Wollstonecraft, 1797–1851. Frankenstein. III. Title. IV. Series.

PZ7.M4784548Fra 2006
[Fic]—dc22

                                                              2005015426

                    2 4 6 8 10 9 7 5 3 1

                Published by Sterling Publishing Co., Inc.
                387 Park Avenue South, New York, NY 10016
                   Copyright © 2006 by Deanna McFadden
                  Illustrations copyright © 2006 by Jamel Akib
                 ^{c}/$_o$ Canadian Manda Group, 165 Dufferin Street
                      Toronto, Ontario, Canada M6K 3H6
       Distributed in Great Britain and Europe by Chris Lloyd at Orca Book
          Services, Stanley House, Fleets Lane, Poole BH15 3AJ, England
          Distributed in Australia by Capricorn Link (Australia) Pty. Ltd.
                   P.O. Box 704, Windsor, NSW 2756, Australia

           Classic Starts is a trademark of Sterling Publishing Co., Inc.

                             Printed in China
                            All rights reserved
                         Designed by Renato Stanisic

                        Sterling ISBN 1-4027-2666-X

          For information about custom editions, special sales, premium and
               corporate purchases, please contact Sterling Special Sales
           Department at 800-805-5489 or specialsales@sterlingpub.com.

CONTENTS

ᘓ

CHAPTER 1:

Captain Robert Walton Meets Victor
Frankenstein 1

CHAPTER 2:

The Story of Victor Frankenstein—
Told in His Own Words 11

CHAPTER 3:

A Tragedy in the Family 20

CHAPTER 4:

Frankenstein Goes to University 26

CHAPTER 5:

The Experiments 31

CHAPTER 6:

Success and Failure 37

CHAPTER 7:

A World Apart from Science 49

CHAPTER 8:

Frankenstein Goes Home 54

CHAPTER 9:

The Trial of Poor Justine 67

CHAPTER 10:

A Long Journey by Foot 77

CHAPTER 11:

The Monster's Story 85

CHAPTER 12:

The Monster's Request 96

CHAPTER 13:

A Journey to England 102

CHAPTER 14:

On to Scotland 106

CHAPTER 15:

The End of My Experiments 112

CHAPTER 16:

The Accusation 118

CHAPTER 17:

The Return to Geneva 129

CHAPTER 18:

The Monster's Revenge 132

CHAPTER 19:

The Last Days of Victor Frankenstein 139

What Do *You* Think? 146

Afterword 150

Classic Starts Library 154

CHAPTER I

Captain Robert Walton Meets Victor Frankenstein

‿∂

The Arctic wind chilled me to the bone as I stood on deck looking out at the frozen land around me. I was in the North Pole. My lifelong dream to come here was now a reality. But at what cost to me and my men? Our ship was trapped on the ice, and we did not know if we would live or die.

I felt foolish. The entire trip had gone terribly wrong. My need to see a part of the world untouched by human beings had turned my trip into a complete disaster. We had ended up so far north because of my own actions. I should have taken the first chance to turn around, but I refused and stubbornly drove on. I didn't care how unhappy it made my crew. My spirit was broken, but I was determined not to quit.

Time passed very slowly. Most days I wished I had a good friend to keep me company. I wanted someone I could talk to during the long, cold nights. I missed having friends more than anything else in the world. Yes, I had a crew of great men on board my ship, but they took orders from me. They were not my friends.

By the next morning, the situation had gotten worse. The ship was completely surrounded by ice. We could do nothing but wait. By mid-afternoon, the fog cleared from the sky and we were able to see more. White snow and ice stretched out from the ship in every direction.

One of the men pointed out a strange sight in the distance. We watched as a sled being pulled

by a large man headed even farther north. The whole crew watched until the man and his sled disappeared on the ice. We turned to one another and asked, "Who was that? What was that?" As far as we knew, there were no people in this part of the world.

The next morning I came out on deck to find my sailors talking to someone over the side of the ship. I leaned over the side and saw a man floating on a piece of ice! All around him were pieces of a broken sled. The ice must have drifted toward us in the night. My men tried to convince him to board our ship so he wouldn't drown.

Something told me that this was not the same man we had seen yesterday. That creature had looked wild and savage, not entirely human. This man was European and he spoke with a thick accent.

"My name is Victor Frankenstein," he shouted

up. "Before I come on board, can you please tell me where you are going?"

"I am Captain Robert Walden," I answered. "This is my ship, and we are on a voyage to the North Pole." Frankenstein was wrapped in many layers of fur, but he still looked cold. "You must come on board. You will freeze out there."

The man nodded. A couple of my sailors threw down some rope and helped him climb on board.

⌒

Frankenstein was almost frozen and in a terrible state! He was pale and thin, and it was clear that he needed a good, warm meal. I could tell that he had been through a hard time. Even before we could get him into a warm cabin, he fainted. We wrapped him up in warm blankets and made him drink a cup of hot tea. He got better slowly and then ate some soup.

When he started to look and feel better, I moved him into my cabin. For some reason, I wanted to help him as much as I could. He tossed and turned in his sleep that first night. There was a great sadness in his eyes, as if he carried the weight of the world on his shoulders.

What a surprise to find a man in the middle of the cold Arctic seas! The sailors wanted to ask him a million questions, but Frankenstein was still sick and I didn't want them to bother him too much. One night after dinner, my first mate, Hardy, came to visit.

"Why did you come so far on such a small sled?" he asked.

Frankenstein stopped smiling and a dark look came into his eyes. "I was chasing someone who ran away from me."

Hardy paused and then said, "Was he traveling on the same kind of sled?"

Frankenstein looked straight at him. "Yes. How did you know that?"

"I think we saw him. We saw a man pulling the same kind of sled across the ice."

"It must be the monster!" Frankenstein yelled. "Which way did he go? Did you see if he made it across the ice? How fast was he going?"

"To the north, but that's all we could see," Hardy answered.

A pale Frankenstein lay back down on the bed.

"That's enough for now!" I said. "He needs his rest. I'll see you in the morning, Hardy." Hardy nodded politely and took his leave.

Frankenstein put his head down on the pillow and said softly, "You must want to know how I got here and what I'm doing. You are polite not to ask."

"You need to get your strength back," I said.

"That's far more important than answering any questions that I may have."

Frankenstein smiled gently at me. "But you saved my life. I am in your debt."

"None of that is important now. You need to rest."

After a quiet moment, Frankenstein asked, "Do you think the ice broke up enough to destroy the other sled? Do you think it is forever lost?"

I told him that it was hard to know for sure because the ice was still solid. Frankenstein fell back into deep thought. "I should like to go back on deck," he said. "I need to watch for that sled."

"No," I said strongly. "You are far too weak. The air is far too cold. I'll get one of my men to watch out for the sled."

"Thank you, Robert." He smiled. "That is so kind."

The next few days passed without event.

Frankenstein's health got better, but he was still weak and spent a lot of time thinking. Despite his sadness, Frankenstein and I talked until late most nights. He became the very friend I so wanted to have on this unlucky journey. All I wanted to do was help him in any way I could. Frankenstein was gentle, wise, and smart. The more I got to know him, the harder it was for me to watch him suffer.

We spoke one night about my Arctic voyage. I told him the whole story and then, for some reason, I grew upset.

I said harshly, "I worry that you think me silly, Frankenstein, for spending all of my money and for pushing my men so hard to get here. I don't know why it is so important to find lands no man has ever seen before. Something inside of me pushes me forward, and I fear nothing will stop me until I have succeeded. I hope you can understand and not think less of me."

Frankenstein's eyes filled with tears when he heard the passion in my voice. He cried out, "Unhappy man! Robert, you must listen carefully to my story. You must know the danger of such strong wishes!"

I was surprised by his outburst. "What story? Frankenstein, what are you talking about?"

"I'm sorry," he said quickly. "Please forgive me for speaking so sharply. Let's talk about something else, shall we?"

At his wish, I changed the subject. We talked about my childhood and my sister in England, and then we went to sleep.

Frankenstein apologized again the next morning, "Robert, I didn't mean to yell. You see, I have lost everything that I loved in this world, including my wife and a dear friend. I want to tell you the whole story. I think it may help you to find your own way."

CHAPTER 2

The Story of Victor Frankenstein— Told in His Own Words

My family comes from Geneva. My father worked hard when he was a young man. So hard, in fact, that he thought of nothing other than his duty to his country. Even love seemed less important. He didn't marry until he was much older.

The true nature of my father's goodness can be seen in the story of how he and my mother came to be married. My father had a dear friend named Beaufort who lost everything and fell on hard times. His life as he knew it was ruined. Beaufort barely had enough money to pay back what he owed before he and his daughter moved to Lucerne. After what had happened, Beaufort did not want to see his friends. He was a proud man who didn't want anyone to see what had become of him.

For ten long years my father looked for his friend. He thought he could make Beaufort come home. He wanted to help him get back on his feet again.

When he finally found him, the situation was far worse than my father had imagined. Beaufort was very sick. His daughter, Caroline, had lost her job because she had to care for him. Together, they had little more than a few cents to rub together. In spite of her hard life, Caroline had remained kind and tender-hearted. My father saw this and fell in love with her.

Beaufort's health grew worse, and he died within a few months. Caroline was very upset. Not only was she poor, but now she was all alone in the world. The day of her father's funeral she cried and cried. What else could she do? She fell down beside the coffin and wept. Her father's death upset her, but she also wondered what would happen to her now.

My father gently lifted her up from her knees. He told her he would bring her back to Geneva and take care of her. They married two years later.

Despite the difference in their ages, my parents had a happy marriage. They loved and respected each other. My father left his job to spend more time with her. Long years caring for her father had made my mother's own health poor. To make her feel better, my parents traveled to the warmer climates of Italy. I was born in Naples, and went with them on all of their trips. My parents loved me completely.

When I was five years old, we visited Lake Como. My mother often helped out with poor families during our travels. She wanted to give back to the world, helping others just as my father had helped her. During our stay on Lake Como, she came across a man and his wife caring for their very large family. A pretty girl with fair skin, blonde hair, and beautiful blue eyes stood out from the rest. She was very sweet, and my mother fell in love with her at once.

My mother visited with the family for many days and spent a lot of time helping the poor mother and her large family. She brought food and clothes, spent time with the children, and had a lovely time. During her stay, my mother watched the beautiful girl closely. She saw her gentle nature, her good manners, and her kind laugh.

One afternoon, my mother and the woman sat talking. The children were playing in front of them, laughing and running.

The woman told my mother that the girl was not her daughter. She had come to the family after her parents had died, leaving her an orphan. The woman said that although the girl had come from a rich family, she had no money now. My mother's heart almost burst at that moment. The girl's story was so similar to her own that she asked if the girl could come to live with us. The woman agreed, and that's how the beautiful Elizabeth Lavenza came to live as a part of our family.

I loved Elizabeth from the first time I saw her. She was a bright and charming child who became my whole world. We never fought or even spoke a mean word to each other. We were very different, but that only made us love one another even more. Elizabeth loved poetry and pretty things: wildflowers, sunshine, and butterflies. I loved science, the natural world, and great thinkers.

The world was a big secret that I wanted to solve. Elizabeth liked how things looked, but I wanted to figure out what made them work. We worked together on all of our studies, spending hours walking about the fields, swimming in the lakes, and reading until all hours of the night.

After my brother Ernest was born, my parents decided to return home for good. We settled into a house in Geneva and bought a small cottage in Bellerive, on the eastern shore of Lake Geneva. We lived in the country far more than in the city. It was a great place to grow up.

Elizabeth and I spent every moment together. We were often joined by our friend, Henry Clerval. He was outgoing and fun-loving. We three were as different as night and day, but we loved one another all the same. The three of us had a very happy childhood. They were my best friends, and I knew we would always be close.

I was a serious child with a very busy mind. I wanted to learn everything and anything. The secrets of Heaven and Earth fascinated me to no end. All I thought about was the world around me: How does it work? Why are we here? How did we all get here? What makes something alive? If my studies made me rough and angry, as they often did, Elizabeth would calm me down. When I became too focused on one subject, Henry made me laugh.

As I grew older, I fell deeper and deeper into my studies. The power of modern science amazed me. I read all the time and filled notebook after notebook with my thoughts. The words of scientists became my life. The more I studied, the more I wanted to know. I read more and more. But the more I read, the more upset I became. No one scientist ever really answered my questions. No one book ever told me exactly what I wanted to know. My mind raced on and on, often all night. My friends and family were kind and ignored my moods. They were supportive even though I spent far too much time with my nose buried in dusty old books.

Nature remained a wonder and a mystery to me. I looked for the secret of life. In truth, I wanted to create life—but I knew I could not do so. Time and money meant little to me. The only thing I cared about was making a great discovery. Maybe I could save humankind from disease. Maybe I could stop a violent death. Perhaps I could finally answer those mysterious questions.

The summer I turned fifteen, we were staying at our summerhouse. A violent and terrible storm came on almost without warning. Thunder burst high in the sky. The heavens were alive with flashes of light. I stood at our back door and stared at the clouds, watching the weather unfold. Suddenly, thunder boomed all around! A split second later, a bolt of lightning crashed from the sky and hit an old oak tree right in front of me. The force of the blast split the tree in half and it burst into flames.

When I went out to look at the tree the next morning, all I found was a burned stump and wood scattered everywhere.

I became very focused on electricity. I needed to know how all that power found its way into a bolt of lightning. I started with the basics and taught myself math. I knew the basics held the key to making my own power. The logic of numbers soon swam around my brain. Maybe if I had known then what would happen to me in later years, I would have stopped—but fate worked in its own way, and the storm happened for a reason.

CHAPTER 3

A Tragedy in the Family

༥ঌ

Years passed and we all grew older. The time soon came for me to go away to school. Just before I was sent to Germany, Elizabeth became very sick with scarlet fever. We were all worried about her. To make matters even worse, the doctor told us to stay away from her. He didn't want anyone else to get sick.

The doctor took good care of Elizabeth. About a week after she got sick, he came to my mother with a sad face and said she had taken a turn for the worse. My mother would not stay away any longer. She ran to Elizabeth's side and nursed her back to health. But this love soon turned to tragedy, and my mother, too, got sick.

The scarlet fever took a hold of my mother, and it would not let go. She grew weaker and weaker. Just before she died, my mother asked to see me and Elizabeth. We sat quietly beside her, each of us holding one of her hands. My mother's face was pale, but she was still beautiful. Her kind eyes looked lovingly upon us, and she smiled as she told us that she wanted to see us married. She knew we were too young to marry right away. Instead, she made us promise to do so when we were older. Elizabeth and I were not surprised by this request. In our hearts, we always knew we would end up together. We were more than happy to tell her we would marry once I finished school.

Then my mother asked Elizabeth to look after our family once she was gone. She wanted

Elizabeth to help raise Ernest and my youngest brother, William, who was just a baby. Elizabeth promised her that she would take the very best care of them.

After saying a tender good-bye to my father, my mother died quietly. We cried and cried. We missed her every single day. But the sad truth is that life goes on. My father soon made it clear that he wanted me to go to school. He understood that I missed my mother and that I wanted to be there for the family, but he said my life should not stop just because I was sad. In the end, my education was more important than my grief.

I didn't want to leave my family when they were still so upset by the sudden death of my mother. Elizabeth took me aside one day and said that I should go.

"Victor," she said quietly, "The sooner you finish school, the sooner we can be married. Your mother's dying wish was to see us happy. You must go away to Germany. It's what she would have wanted."

In my heart, I knew Elizabeth was right. She was right about so many things. Elizabeth became the rock upon which we all depended. She was strong, and took good care of my father and brothers. She loved us with her kind and tender heart. My affections for her grew greater as each day passed. I loved her deeply. She was such a giving person. It was much easier for me to leave knowing that my family was in her hands.

The night before I left for Germany, Henry, Elizabeth, and I sat in the kitchen with hot chocolate and talked. We remembered stories from our childhood. We told each other our dreams. No one wanted to go to bed, so we stayed up all night. We drank mug after mug of the warm, sweet drink on and on into the night. When the sun rose the next morning, no one wanted to say good-bye.

A couple hours later, my bags were packed and in the carriage. Finally it was time for me to leave. My father gave me a long hug. I made Elizabeth promise to write to me all the time. Ernest held back his tears and held baby William tightly. Henry gave me his strongest handshake. They gave me a wonderful, loving send-off.

I stepped into the carriage and called out, "Don't worry all! I shall see you soon!"

With those words, I started the long journey to Germany. I sat back and looked out the carriage window as my house grew smaller and smaller in the distance. For the first time in my life, I was completely alone.

CHAPTER 4

Frankenstein Goes to University

❧

It took three long days of traveling to get to Ingolstadt. The beauty of the town around the school was lost to me because I was so tired. I spent much of that first week in my room getting ready for my classes.

Monday came and I took my letter of introduction around to the teachers. My new science teacher greeted me coldly. His name was Professor Krempe. With his glasses sitting on the end of his nose, he asked what I had already studied. I told him about all the reading I had done when I was younger. I also told him how I learned everything I could about the natural world and then started to teach myself mathematics. When he learned which scientists I had been reading, he started to yell!

"Nonsense!" he shouted. "All nonsense!" He dipped a pen into ink and wrote quickly for a moment.

"Start here," he told me. "Commit these books to memory. You must start over as of today."

I took the piece of paper he held out to me. He looked at me firmly and continued, "I will teach you natural science starting next Monday. Every other day you will be with Professor Waldman. He will teach you chemistry. That is all."

"Thank you, professor," I said quietly, "I will do my best to get caught up before then."

Professor Krempe nodded, and I left his office. It upset me that I was so far behind.

I started classes the next week. Professor Waldman was an older man. His brown hair had started to turn gray by his ears. Although he wasn't very tall, he certainly had a big, booming voice.

Our first lesson began with the history of chemistry. The professor explained how much science had changed over the years: "Great progress is being made. With the help of microscopes, modern scientists are seeing a world we barely even knew existed before today."

His voice carried through the classroom: "These scientists have discovered how and why blood runs through the body. They know what makes up the air we breathe. They can grab thunder from heaven. They can make the Earth shake. The possibilities of science today are as endless as the minds that pursue them."

He paused for a moment and then continued, "You young students are the next group of great thinkers."

My mind raced. *Yes,* I thought to myself, *Yes! Yes! I, Victor Frankenstein, will find the truth behind the world's greatest mysteries!* Those thoughts set my fate. My dreams flowed like a great river. Nothing could stop me. I became Professor Waldman's best student. I never missed a single class and listened to his every word.

One day I decided to visit him at home. I wanted extra reading. The professor was happy to see me. He seemed very different at home.

"How can I help you, Victor?" he asked quietly. We sat in his living room, drank coffee, and talked about chemistry for a long time.

I explained, "I need to learn everything I can about chemistry, sir. Do you have extra reading or experiments I can do?"

"Young man, I am glad to hear how eager you are to learn! But science isn't just chemistry. To be a really good scientist, you need to know about all different kinds of science, including math."

I replied, "Yes, sir. I'm willing to learn anything and everything I need to know to be a great scientist!"

Professor Waldman was then kind enough to show me his laboratory. The machines were amazing! He showed me his equipment, and told me how to build my own laboratory. Toward the end of our visit, he gave me the list of books I was looking for. What a wonderful day it was! It had such an effect on me—it decided my destiny.

CHAPTER 5

The Experiments

～

For the next two years, school was my whole world. My progress excited Professor Waldman. The best part of science was the many discoveries we made. By the end of my classes, I had actually improved many of the instruments we used in our daily work. I finished school knowing that my education was a success.

Now that school was done, I had a decision to make. I could go home and marry Elizabeth, or I could stay and continue my work in the lab. I still had questions about the human body and how it worked. What gives a creature life? It was a hard question, but I needed to know the answer. All of the tools to make such a great discovery were here in my laboratory. Everything the school had to offer was at my fingertips. I decided not to go home just yet. Instead, I stayed in Ingolstadt.

In order to discover the secrets of life, I needed to learn more about death. A gloomy thought indeed, but it made sense to me at the time. I started to study the human body and looked at what happens to the body after life has left it.

Things that might upset other people didn't seem to bother me at all. I wasn't scared of ghosts or working late in graveyards. I spent hour upon hour in tombs with the bodies, watching every stage of their changes. The differences between life and death struck me, and I noted every single one.

Time went by quickly. I barely noticed weeks and months slipping away. Then one day, I made the most amazing discovery. After a lot of thought and hard work, I discovered I could give life to lifeless matter. Like a magic scene, these findings opened up a whole new world of possibility to me.

"I've done it!" I exclaimed. "It works!"

It took me a minute to catch my breath. I sat down on a chair beside my experiment and thought about what to do now. How should I use this discovery? Should I make a man like myself? Or should I make a smaller animal, something simple?

No, I thought. *What does the world need? Not another animal. No, science would be served best if I created a man. What would people think?!*

My imagination flew. This first success made me think I could do anything I set my mind to. This man would need to be perfect. It took me many months to gather everything I needed. My final goal drove me along like a hurricane.

Neither life nor death could stop me. A new species would have me as its maker.

I devoted all of my time to my work. My cheeks grew pale from spending too much time inside, and my body grew thin because I wasn't eating enough. My mind raced day and night. I barely stopped to sleep. I spent long nights working by moonlight and candlelight. I was full of energy.

My laboratory, which was on the second floor of my apartment, was separated from all of the other apartments by a long, creeping stairway. It was for the best. The last thing that I wanted was for anyone else to find my work. I had the feeling that people wouldn't understand what I was doing and why.

Bottles of liquid bubbled everywhere. They would terrify a visitor. There were eyeballs, ears, and other body parts—many of which I had taken from the local hospital—lying everywhere. I used any parts I could get my hands on. The most important thing was building this man. Nothing else mattered.

Winter turned to spring, and then spring turned to summer. The winds became warm and the flowers bloomed. The changes in the weather were lost on me. I did not see any of them. All I could see was my work. Nothing could tear me away, not even the thought of my friends and family. Not even the thought of my beautiful Elizabeth.

I knew my family was upset with me. I hadn't sent them a letter in months. Deep down, I knew they would forgive me. They knew I loved them. I told myself that all great discoveries came from great sacrifices. The letters from home piled up in my living room, unopened and unread.

Summer turned to fall. The world outside my laboratory window changed again. Seasons that I used to love and time that I used to cherish went by in a flash. A slow burning fever started to bother me most nights. My nerves were worn. The only thing that kept me going was the thought of success.

Soon, I thought one evening. *Soon he will be alive.*

CHAPTER 6

Success and Failure

ᴄᴏ

One night, the rain fell steadily outside the windows of my laboratory. The cold November air chilled me to the bone. I could hardly believe it myself, but I was finished. I collected the instruments around me and tried to bring my creature to life. My candle was nearly burnt down. I felt weak and tired. Then, in the flicker of the half-light, I saw the creature open his dull yellow eyes. A breath escaped his lips. His arms and legs moved. He was alive!

Almost at once I began to cry. They were not

tears of joy, though, as you might expect. No, I cried with misery and regret.

"What have I done?!" I cried out. "What a disaster!"

I had chosen his parts so carefully, but it had all gone so terribly wrong. How can I describe the horror I felt? I had seen him before I brought him to life, but I had not seen that he was so ugly. Now he was alive, and there was nothing more I could do but be sorry for my actions.

His limbs were the right size, but his watery, pale eyes were awful. His yellow-looking skin barely covered his muscles and veins. His hair was black, even flowing, and his teeth were white and pearly—but his lips were thin and black.

I had spent two years building this creature. Now that I was finished, the glory of my dream disappeared like the light from my candle. My heart filled with horror and disgust. I could not bear to look at him. I rushed out of the lab and threw myself on my bed. Rest did not come easily. My dreams were awful. They were full of terrible pictures: my poor, suffering mother and a sick Elizabeth.

When I woke up in a terrible sweat, the monster was standing above me! He made a noise, maybe an attempt to speak. Then he held out one giant hand to grab me, but I ran out of the room as fast as I could. I ran down the stairs, out the door, and into the street. I stopped to see if he was following me, and then I ran off into town.

I spent the rest of the night walking the streets of Ingolstadt, listening for footsteps behind me. What did he want from me, the awful creature? The frightening monster of my own creation haunted me that night. Every noise scared me and made me think the body to which I had so wrongly given life was about to catch me. I imagined his big, awful hands around my neck. How had everything had turned out so bad? My dream had turned into a living nightmare.

I walked all through the night in the pouring rain. I did not dare return to my apartment. Eventually I ended up at an inn on the other side of town, where a Swiss coach was parked. The door flew open and there stood Henry Clerval, my dear friend.

"Victor!" he shouted. "I am so glad to see you! What luck. How could you have known to meet my carriage?"

I forgot my unhappiness for a moment, and the monster vanished. The cool morning air blew all of my mistakes away. For the first time in months, I thought about something other than my experiments.

"Henry!" I gave my friend a big hug. "No, I didn't know you were coming. What are you doing here? I'm so happy to see you!"

He smiled. "My father finally allowed me to come to school. Can you believe it?"

"That's wonderful!" I replied. "How is my family? You must have brought news from home with you. How is Elizabeth? My father? My brothers?"

"Not to worry, Victor." He said. "They are all well. They wish you would write more, though." He punched me playfully on the shoulder, and then took a good look at me. "My, you are thin and pale. Are you sick?"

"I've been working day and night on an experiment." I forgot everything that had happened the night before and said quickly, "Let's go back to my rooms for a nice breakfast!"

We took Henry's carriage back to my apartment. As we approached my building, a fear came over me. What if the monster was still there? What would I do then? Henry could not see it. What would he think of me?

The carriage stopped in front of my door, and Henry said good-bye to the driver. We gathered his bags and stepped into my front hallway. "Wait down here for just a minute," I said. "I need to clean up quickly."

"Oh Victor, I don't care about a mess. I'm tired and want to sit somewhere that doesn't move."

I begged, "Please, just one minute, okay?" I darted up the stairs. A cold shiver ran down my spine as I arrived at my door. Gathering up all my courage, I threw it wide open. I expected a ghost, knowing now that such fears would haunt me. A long sigh escaped my lips as I found the rooms to be empty. The awful monster was gone!

"Henry," I shouted down the stairs, "come on upstairs!

The woman in charge of my apartment brought us a large breakfast. We ate together and Henry told me all about his trip. The coach from Geneva was quite an adventure! He went on and on about the funny people he had met along the way. I smiled and listened to his stories. Oh, how I missed my friend Henry! After spending so many months locked away in my laboratory, I had forgotten the simple joys of friendship.

After we finished eating, I couldn't sit still. Something in me shook loose and I could not control myself. I had too much energy. I jumped over chairs, waving my hands around wildly and giggling uncontrollably. My strange behavior made Henry uncomfortable.

"Victor," he shouted. "Sit still for a minute. You're making me nervous with all your twitching and stuff. What's the matter with you?"

"Nothing!" I said. "I'm terrific!" I started laughing and couldn't stop.

Then, for a split second, I thought I saw the monster. "Do not ask me!" I cried. I threw my hands over my eyes and screamed. "He knows!"

I yelled. "He knows! Oh, save me! Oh, save me!" In my mind, the monster had grabbed me and was shaking me all about. I struggled against him and then I fell down to the floor.

Henry rushed toward me. He must have helped me to my bed, but I have no memory of it. I fell into a fever that lasted for some time. Henry took good care of me and decided not to tell my family right away because he knew they would be very worried. One could not ask for a better friend.

Months went by but I didn't notice. Terrible thoughts came to me in my dreams. Awful sights of the monster I had created. Fear of what I had done and could never undo. I tossed and turned night after night. Henry stayed by my side night and day. He fed me soup and read to me. The fever held on and there were days when I couldn't even sit up in bed. My room became my entire world. My window the only way I knew the world was still there.

Slowly, after many starts, I began to feel better. Germany was now in the full bloom of spring. Birds sang in the trees and the flowers started to bloom. I could hardly believe that I had been sick all winter. Where did all the time go? What happened to the monster? What had I done? I pushed those thoughts out of my mind and tried to think about my life before my experiments. How I enjoyed being outside. How Henry, Elizabeth, and I had so much fun when we were children. Now, with the weather being so nice, my mood got a great deal better.

"Henry!" I said one morning. "You are so good to me. You were supposed to start school already, but you've spent the whole season taking care of me." He smiled but didn't say anything, so I continued, "How will I ever pay back this kindness?"

"There's no need." He replied. "All you need to do is get well. That's all that matters." He paused for a minute and then said, "But there is one thing you can help me with."

I shook under my sheets. Maybe he wanted to know about my lab? Maybe he saw evidence of the monster somewhere? Maybe he knew everything! I couldn't bear it if Henry found out! What would he think of me? Would he tell my family? Would they be disappointed in me, too?

Henry noticed my panic. He begged, "Please don't be upset. I want you to send a letter home. Your family wants to hear from you. They are worried about your health."

I sighed, "Is that all?" I kicked off my sheets and sat up in bed. "Of course! I don't want them to worry anymore now that I'm so much better."

Henry walked to the table and said, "There's a letter here from Elizabeth. I'll go out for a while and let you read it by yourself."

Henry smiled kindly at me, put on his hat, and

left the room. I sat down at my table and slowly opened the letter, not knowing what to expect. It had been so long since I had read a letter from my family. My heart raced just thinking about how happy I was to hear from them.

CHAPTER 7

A World Apart from Science

In her letter, Elizabeth begged me to write home, even one word. It had been so long since they had heard from me. She told me she had had to convince my father not to come to Germany to get me! In her sweet writing, she told me how she wanted to come to Ingolstadt, too, but she had to look after the house and my brothers.

The words on the page gave me only good news. My brother Ernest had just turned sixteen. She told me all about how he wanted to enter the Foreign Service, just like our father.

How proud I would be of him, she wrote, for being such a good Swiss citizen! She wrote on about how well the children's nanny, Justine, was doing, and how pleased she was to have a female friend around.

"We are like sisters!" she wrote. *"I am so happy to have her here with me, especially because William is such a handful!"*

She filled the rest of the letter with local news about our friends and neighbors. I enjoyed every word. Elizabeth finished the letter by asking me again to write home, for her sake. What a sweet, sweet girl. I missed her so much at that moment. I felt so foolish for getting so caught up in my miserable work. I had forgotten what was important in the world—the love of friends and family.

I wrote back to her at once. I told her how much I missed her and how much I loved her. When I was finished, I put the letter in that day's post.

Two more weeks passed and I was finally able to leave my room. It was a good thing, too, because Henry was about to start his classes and I could show him around the school.

We spent a day walking around. I introduced Henry to everyone I knew. I took him around to all of my old science buildings and showed him all of my old classrooms. When we got to the laboratory, I felt the blood drain from my face. Seeing all the equipment again greatly bothered me. Henry noticed I was upset and kindly helped me outside. I know he wanted me to tell him what was wrong, but I just couldn't do it. The truth was too awful.

Henry started school within a couple of days. He had no interest in science at all. Instead, he wanted to learn all about the different languages of the world. Never one to just rest, I decided to study them, too.

We spent the summer like this, reading and

studying together. It was good to keep my mind busy. I sent word to my father that I would be coming home to Geneva in the fall. But when it came time for me to leave, the weather turned poor and I was forced to stay in Ingolstadt for the season.

It was May before the roads were safe to drive. Once again, the spring weather made me feel much better. A year had passed since my fit, and I was stronger than ever. I was feeling so well, in fact, that Henry suggested we take a walking tour of the country around the school. I thought it was a great idea. I could say goodbye to the land I had called home for the past few years.

We traveled around for two weeks. The fresh air did my heart and lungs good. I had spent far too long in my laboratory with my nose buried in books and experiments. I had forgotten how much I enjoyed just being outside. The flowers bloomed, and their beauty amazed me. The trees smelled wonderful. The lake shone. I forgot the last, miserable year.

Henry and I walked and talked, and then walked and talked some more. We got along so well, and his good company made me very happy. I was reminded of who I was before coming to school, before I played with nature, and before I made the mistake of creating an awful monster.

We got back to school on a Sunday afternoon. We met only cheerful people on the road back to Ingolstadt. My spirits flew. There was a spring in my step. My heart was full of joy.

CHAPTER 8

Frankenstein Goes Home

⌁

A letter from my father was waiting for me when I got home. I happily tore it open and found that it contained bad news. I read my father's words slowly: *"There is no easy way for me to tell you this, but your brother William is dead."*

Tears sprang to my eyes. The family had taken their usual walk after dinner. The evening was warm and calm, so they decided to stay out longer than usual. My father and Elizabeth walked behind William and Ernest. Instead of trying to catch up to them, they decided to sit and wait for the boys to return. When Ernest found them, he explained that William had run off to hide and he couldn't find him anywhere.

My father and Elizabeth were scared. They started looking for him right away. They spent hours and hours looking, but they couldn't find him. The police were called and a search party was put together. Everyone spent the night looking for William. They searched high and low, every place a small boy would hide, but with no luck. No one said anything, but they all feared something terrible had happened to poor William. It was an awful night for Elizabeth, my father wrote.

In the early hours of the morning, my father discovered my brother. His worst fears had come true. My brother was no longer alive. My father was very upset. Everyone was.

"Come home, Victor," my father's letter continued. *"You are the only person who can help Elizabeth through this hard time."*

Elizabeth had taken the news harder than any other member of the family—she thought it was her fault! That morning, she had given William a gold locket that had belonged to our mother. She thought the jewelry must have been the cause of the terrible accident. William must have gotten in the way of a thief trying to take the locket. If she had never given it to him, he would still be alive.

I put the letter on the table and started to cry.

"Victor," Henry said, "what's wrong? Has something happened?"

I couldn't speak, so I handed him the letter. "Oh, no!" Henry exclaimed. "What are you going to do?"

"I must go home right away," I answered. "My family needs me, and I need to be with them."

I quickly packed a bag. There was little time to be neat. I threw things in every which way, trying not to think about my poor brother. Henry helped me. He asked the woman in charge of the apartment to pack a lunch, which she did happily. Together we organized my books, papers, and clothes for the trip back to Geneva.

Henry was going to stay on in my rooms at Ingolstadt. He had to continue with his studies, and that was fine with me. I did, however, lock my laboratory and take the key with me. I didn't want Henry going in there while I was gone.

We walked slowly and with heavy hearts to the carriage. Henry gave me a long hug and said a tearful goodbye. "Tell your family I send my love, Victor. I am so sorry for what happened."

"I will, Henry. You are a good friend. I will miss you terribly."

There was nothing else to say, so I climbed on board. The driver called out to the horses and we were away. I turned around to look out the window at Henry. He stood there long after the carriage rode away, waving. Tears fell down my face.

I wept for my dear, sweet brother. I thought of my mother. And I felt sorry for myself, how I had let my family down. How I should have been there for them during this awful time. I just hoped it wasn't too late.

The carriage was warm and comfortable, but my three-day trip was full of pain. Six years had passed since I had seen my hometown. When I saw the top of Mont Blanc, I began to cry. My country, my beloved country! As we drew closer to home, the day turned to night. The city gates were closed by the time we arrived in Geneva. The carriage turned around and brought me to Secheron, a small town about a mile away, where I stayed the night.

When I stepped out of the carriage and stretched, I looked up and saw a clear sky with lots of stars. The weather was in my favor. My legs were restless from so much traveling, and I knew

I would never sleep. I decided to visit the spot where my father had found William.

With the city gates closed, I needed to cross Lake Geneva by boat. Luckily, I could borrow one from the inn where I was staying. During my short trip, the weather quickly took a turn for the worse. Lightning flashed in the sky that had been calm just minutes before. Rain started to fall. I rowed as hard as I could to get to land. The heavens clouded up, and it was hard to see my way. Thunder burst overhead as I pressed on toward land.

I landed on the beach and dragged the boat out of the water. I tied it up, and ran into the woods. I had a basic idea from my father's letter of where the crime had taken place, and started off in that direction. "Oh, William!" I exclaimed. "You poor, darling boy." As these words left my lips, I saw a figure run away from behind the trees. I stood completely still. Could it be? Yes! It was the monster, that awful creature to whom I had given life. At once, I knew he was the one who was guilty. He alone took William's life. Oh, cursed monster!

My teeth started to chatter. My legs felt weak. I leaned on a tree for support and tried to take a deep breath. I watched as the creature quickly ran away. I started to chase after him even though my legs felt funny. Small brushes hit my legs, and I almost tripped on a number of rocks. I ran as fast as I could. The monster jumped over fallen trees and ducked under branches. I tried as hard as I could, but I couldn't catch him. He reached the top of the small forest and disappeared.

I sank down beside a tree as the rain continued. I was getting wetter and wetter, but

I couldn't move. What did the monster want? Was this his first crime? How many other people had he hurt?

I spent a cold, wet night in the open air. When day dawned, I made my way back to the inn and returned the boat. I decided to walk the rest of the way home. It would give me time to think. The carriage was to bring my bags to my home. My mind raced. How could I explain to my father what had happened? How could I tell him that I had created a man, a monster, from parts? How could I tell him that this monster had killed William and was hiding somewhere on Mont Blanc? I would sound like a crazy person. No, I needed to keep my secret to myself for now. There was no other choice.

As I walked up our road, I noticed that very little had changed. The house looked and felt the same, and that was comforting. I quietly opened the front door and walked inside. I found my brother Ernest already awake and sitting in the living room.

"Welcome home, Victor!" He smiled faintly. "I'm sorry your homecoming is so sad." When I opened up my arms, Ernest almost fell into them and started to cry. I was in pain, too. If I had not driven myself so hard this never would have happened. It's all my fault. My two hands had ruined this lovely home. My work had caused the sadness my family now felt.

"How are Father and Elizabeth?" I asked him.

Ernest wiped his eyes and tried to stand up strong. "They are sad, but now that the criminal has been caught—"

"Caught?" I interrupted. "What do you mean? I saw him walking free last night."

My brother looked confused. "No," he said, "it's Justine, William's nanny. She's been accused and is in jail as we speak. They arrested her last night."

"Justine?" Now it was my turn to be confused. "That sweet girl? No, she's not guilty. There must be some mistake."

Ernest sat down on the couch and explained what happened. After my father returned with the bad news, Justine fell ill. Her fever continued for days. My father called the doctor, but he couldn't find anything wrong with her. One of the maids had found our mother's locket in the pocket of her skirt. She was taking Justine's clothes to be cleaned when it fell out. The maid didn't say anything to the family, but went straight to the police.

"When they came to question her, Justine simply cried," my brother continued. "She was so confused and upset that they decided she must be guilty."

My father came in as we were talking. He looked worn down and tired, but he smiled warmly when he saw me.

"My son," he said, "I am glad you're home." I hugged him tightly.

"Father!" Ernest exclaimed. "Victor knows who killed William—"

"Alas," my father said, "so do we, and I would have much rather not known. It's upsetting to think that someone we treated like family could do something so terrible."

"But Father," I said, "Justine is innocent." I longed to tell him everything about the monster and about how my experiment had gone so very wrong. But I just couldn't, not without him being angry with me.

"Well, I hope you are right," he said. "Her trial starts today."

I looked up to see Elizabeth come into the room. Time had been kind to her. In spite of her obvious sadness, she had grown from a lovely young girl into a beautiful woman. The love I had for her swelled my heart.

We embraced. Elizabeth, like my father and brother, said she was glad I was home. Ernest quickly told her about our conversation.

Elizabeth turned to me. "Victor, we must save Justine. I can't believe she did it. I won't believe she did it!" She sat down on the couch, took her handkerchief out of her pocket, and wiped away her tears.

"She's such a sweet girl," Elizabeth continued, "And she loved William as if he were her own brother. There is no way she could have hurt him. I can't imagine what the police are thinking!"

Elizabeth started to cry again and I put my hand on her shoulder. "Elizabeth, please be still. Justine is innocent. There's nothing to be afraid of. She won't be going to jail." I made my self a silent promise to do everything I could to make up for all of my actions. To make up for what I have put my family through. They didn't deserve to suffer because I had made so many mistakes.

"There, there," I said to Elizabeth, "Everything is going to be okay." I smiled warmly at her and held her hand, "I promise."

My father added, "We must trust our legal system to do the right thing. The truth will come out, that's certain."

With those final words, my family and I went into the dining room for breakfast. It was a silent meal. In my heart I knew they were thinking about poor William and about how sad my mother would have been if she were here. But my mind kept coming back to one chilling thought: Where was the monster now?

CHAPTER 9

The Trial of Poor Justine

⚬

The trial started at eleven o'clock that morning. The whole family went to court. Ernest and I went for support. My father and Elizabeth went to tell the court what a good person Justine was. A sour mood filled me with anger and regret. Justine should be living a good life. She was a loyal, kind person. She shouldn't be on trial for murder! But I couldn't tell anyone what I knew. I would be thought of as a madman, and sent away for the rest of my life. What good would that serve?

Justine sat in the box for the accused. She looked pale, but calm. A tear slipped down her cheek when she saw our family enter the courtroom.

The bailiff called the room to order and the trial began. The evidence built against the poor girl. The court said she had been out all night. A market woman had seen her early the next morning not far from where they found William. The woman asked Justine what she had been doing, but all she got was a confused answer. The fact that the maid had found the missing locket in Justine's clothes was still the strongest piece of evidence.

The judge called upon Justine to speak in her own defense. Her voice was clear, but it was obvious that she was deeply troubled.

"I am entirely innocent. I know I can say it, but you do not have to believe me. My good character should also be taken as evidence."

She told the court that Elizabeth had given her permission to visit with her aunt the day my brother was killed. On her way back to Geneva, she met a man who asked if she had seen a young boy who was missing. When Justine realized that it was William who could not be found, she had joined the search party. Over the next few hours, Justine searched the woods high and low for my brother.

Justine went on to tell the court that it was very late when she finally stopped looking. By that time, the city gates were closed. Justine did not know what to do, so she asked a kindly old man if she could sleep in his barn.

She spent a cold, scary night lying on some hay in the barn near town. Every noise woke her up and she slept very little. When the market woman found her, she was confused because she hadn't slept. If she had walked by where they found William, she didn't do it on purpose. But the locket? Justine cried. She didn't know how it got into her pocket—it was the one thing she just couldn't explain.

Several townspeople spoke up next. Many knew Justine to be a good person, but they believed the evidence. They thought she was guilty. My father told the court how well Justine had served our family. Next, Elizabeth was called to the stand. She told the court that the girl would never do anything to harm the children she nursed.

"She is perfectly innocent," Elizabeth swore.

Elizabeth's speech moved many in the audience. Justine looked thankful for her kind words and put on a brave face. However, the judge did not look at all convinced. The jury cast their votes and we waited patiently while they were counted.

The bailiff came back into the courtroom and announced that Justine was guilty! I felt a great sense of despair. Justine was sentenced to spend the rest of her life in jail. Elizabeth collapsed beside me and started to cry. I did my best to comfort her, in spite of the aches in my own heart.

Everything was my fault! My hands alone had built that monster. I could not stop my mind from turning those awful memories over and over. What if this wasn't the last of the monster's evil actions? What if my brother and Justine were just the first victims of my own creation?

I was free and alive while Justine was in jail and my brother was dead. Nothing could remove the pain in my soul. My blind need for a great discovery had come at such a high price. Instead of finding hope in my work, I now felt nothing but sadness.

The events of the past few weeks took their toll on my already weak body. Nothing but a long talk with my father could tear me away from my grief.

"My son," he said one afternoon when he

noticed that I was sitting in the corner just staring out the window, "no one could have loved a child as much as I loved your brother, but we cannot spend all of our days staring blankly out of windows. We are all unhappy. You owe it to both Justine and your brother to be useful. Without that, no man is fit for society."

He spoke the truth, but my father's words meant little to me.

We decided to spend time at our summer house in Bellerive. The fact that the city gates closed early in the evening made me feel trapped. I was glad to be in the country and be able to roam free.

I would leave the house most nights while the rest of the family was sleeping. I would take the boat and spend many hours on the water. Sometimes, I would leave the sail up and make my way with a purpose. But more often than not, I would let the water carry the boat wherever it wanted to go. I would lie in the bottom and stare up at the stars. The simple beauty of the sky would bring me to tears. I cried openly, knowing that no one but the frogs and the fish could hear or see me.

I lived in fear day in and day out, knowing the monster was still alive. What if he did something else? How could I live with myself? What if he hurt someone else I loved? These thoughts made me so angry that I ground my teeth and screamed at the top of my lungs.

In those moments, all I thought about was taking back the gift I had given him. If I could return my world to the way it had been before my experiment, maybe I could make things right again. My thoughts were evil. But what was worse? Creating him or stopping more bad things from happening? It was a moral dilemma of the first degree.

Everyone in our house was sad. My father

tried to be strong, but we could all tell he wasn't the same. Elizabeth had tears in her eyes almost every day. For the sake of them both, I tried to be strong on the outside and hide my inner pain.

In the middle of our grief, my brother Ernest left. We wished him well as he entered the Foreign Service. It's strange how life repeats itself. Just a few years ago I had left home after we lost our mother. Now Ernest left just after another loss.

One day, Elizabeth and I sat talking. She told me she was upset about how things had turned out. "The fate of poor Justine makes me think the world is an awful place. Before now, bad things only happened in books. Now, our lives are full of sadness. Justine was innocent, but she went to jail. How is that fair?"

Oh, my lovely Elizabeth! It hurt me so much to hear her so upset. I was the cause of all of these troubles, not because I actually did them, but because I created the monster. My face became an ashy color. Elizabeth saw the color drain from my cheeks.

She grabbed my hands and said, "I'm sorry, my love. I didn't mean to upset you." She held them tightly. "Everything will be okay. Maybe not today, but it will be soon. I promise."

I smiled at her kindly, but I didn't feel any better. In the back of my mind, I knew it was far from over.

"I'm sorry, Elizabeth. I need to be alone right now." I rose from the couch and went up to my room. I wanted to tell her the truth. To explain how everything was my fault. But I couldn't bring myself to do it.

Hours later, I decided the only thing that would make me feel better was a long hike through the Alps. Maybe if I took another trip like the one with Henry, I could get over what had happened to poor William and Justine.

CHAPTER 10

A Long Journey by Foot

⌒

The next morning, just as the sun was starting to rise, I quietly slipped out the front door, careful not to wake anyone. I started off with a firm step toward the Alpine slopes. My hope was that the crisp, cool mountain air would clear my head. Before long I was headed up the path to Chamonix—a small town built in a beautiful valley.

The roads felt good under my boots. The weather was fair and bright. The weight on my shoulders lessened the farther I traveled into the mountains. They were so tall on either side of me! They looked like they had giant pyramids made of snow sitting on top of each of them. The mighty slopes were amazing. I never tired of looking at them, no matter how many times I walked this way. There was something magical about my country. I loved traveling through the Alps.

It took me a day to get to Chamonix. There was a nice inn where I found a room to stay for the night. The minute I put my head on the pillow, I fell into a deep sleep.

The next morning I got up and started off again. I roamed through the Chamonix Valley with the sounds of nature all around. Wind rustled through the trees and the stream bubbled as the water ran downhill. The trip did me good, but I was still troubled. I decided to stay another day before going back home.

It rained the next day, but I didn't want to

spend the day inside. What was a storm to me? I had been through much worse. I borrowed a mule from the inn so I could hike to the top of Montenvers. The glaciers at the peak were incredible. I really wanted to see them that day. I knew that view alone would make me feel better.

The path going up the mountain was difficult, but not impossible. Pine trees lined the way. The trail twisted and turned as the mule and I made our way up. The valley sat far below us. There were warm cottages, and I could see fires burning. The people inside would be gladly going about their days.

Those are the signs of a wonderful life, I thought. *Would I ever be that happy?*

So much had happened in my life. My thoughts drifted back over the events of the past few years as I rode up higher and higher. The death of my mother, my time at school, my awful experiment, seeing the monster, poor William, innocent Justine—I knew things would never be the same. I would never again be that boy looking with wonder at a bolt of lightning.

Rain poured down from the sky, but I kept walking. By the time I reached the top of Montenvers, it was nearly noon. I left the mule to rest by the path and started off on my own. I hiked for another couple of hours and then sat down on a rock that overlooked the sea of ice. After resting there for a while, I figured I had enough energy to cross the glacier. It took me two hours to reach the other side, but the exercise did me good.

I turned around and took a good look at the mountains. The glory of Montenvers rose in the distance, with the great Mont Blanc just behind it. I called out to the sky, "Please, just let me be happy! Please, just let me put all this behind me. I can't go on like this! I really can't."

As I said these words, I saw a man running quickly across the glacier. He flew over places where I had taken my time being careful not to fall. When I got a closer look, I saw that he was much, much taller than a man.

No! I thought. *It can't be.* I felt faint and almost fell over, but the cool air of the glacier steadied me. It was the monster! He came running toward me. I shook with a mixture of rage and fear.

"Monster!" I screamed. "How dare you come near me after what you've done! Are you not afraid of me? Do you not see my anger?"

He shouted back, "I know you hate me. Everyone hates me, wherever I go. I am miserable. But you created me and you alone are tied to me."

He came closer and continued, "I want you to do something for me. If you agree, I will leave you alone. If you do not agree, I will make your life very unhappy."

"How dare you!" I screamed. "How dare you!" I raced across to where he was standing, with my fists raised. He easily stepped out of my way and I fell onto the ice. I got up and brushed the snow from my pants.

The monster said, "Do not act foolishly. For the past two years I have seen happiness all around me, but none has come to me. I have seen people love and be loved, but no one has loved me. I have learned to speak, to read, to think clearly, and still people reject me. You created me, Frankenstein, and now you must bless my life as your life has been blessed—with people who love you."

"Be gone!" I roared. "We are enemies, Monster. It doesn't matter that I created you."

He hung his head for a minute. "How can I make you listen? How can I make you understand? Frankenstein, I am all alone in this world. If my creator despises me, how can I expect anyone else to feel differently?"

His voice cracked as he continued, "The cold ice and snow of these mountains are my home now. I live a rough life. Only you have the power to help me. Please, just listen to my story. When you have heard it all, then you can judge me."

I clasped my hands over my ears and shook my head. "No," I shouted, "No! I don't want to listen to you. You have made my life miserable. Just leave, and never talk to me again."

"Not until you hear my story," he insisted. "Not until you know what I need to ask you and what I want you to do. Frankenstein, please, it's very cold. This weather isn't good for you—you may get sick. Come with me to my hut."

As I thought about his offer for a moment, he spoke again. "My life is still in your hands. You alone can decide whether or not I leave forever and never hurt those you love again."

He turned and started back across the glacier. I slowly followed him across the ice. I hated him, but I owed him this much—I would listen to his story.

CHAPTER 11

The Monster's Story

The monster and I hiked slowly to his hut. It was a rough looking building. We went inside and sat beside a warm fire. The flames made the monster's pale face glow with a strange light. He started the story at the beginning of his life, at that fateful moment when I left him.

"It's hard for me to remember the first few days of my life. They are all one big blur. I saw, felt, heard, and smelled all at the same time. My senses were all mixed up."

I interrupted him to ask, "Your senses came all at once? That must have been confusing."

"At first, yes, but then I learned to tell them apart. The light hurt my eyes and I had to keep them closed for a long time. After I left your apartment, I found my way into a forest near Ingolstadt. I lay down beside a stream and slept. Hours later, I woke up because my stomach hurt and my throat was sore. I found I could drink the water in the stream, and it was wonderful. Then I ate some berries and roots that I found in the forest. My stomach isn't like yours, Frankenstein. It does quite well with a rough diet."

He shifted away from the fire as it heated up the room. I didn't know what to think, or even what to say, so I just listened.

"It was dark and cold when I woke up. The clothes I wore weren't warm enough for the weather. I was so unhappy. My arms and legs ached, and my mind spun with many thoughts—none of which I understood. So I sat down and cried. I didn't know what else to do.

"The moon lit up the sky, and I felt better. I stood up and found an old cloak someone had thrown away under a tree. During the time when I felt everything at once, the only thing that made me feel better was the sight of the moon. It calmed me down."

"How long did you stay in the forest?" I asked.

"For many days—I had nowhere else to go. I stayed until I could calm my senses and tell one apart from the other."

The monster cleared his throat before he continued. "One day, when it was really cold, I went for a long walk. A group of travelers had left behind a fire. When I sat down beside it, I was surprised to feel the heat. I put my hand right in the middle of it! How the pain that caused surprised me!"

He held up his hand so I could see the scar

from the burn. Then, he said, "I examined the fire closely and saw that it was made of wood. I went and gathered some more so I could keep the fire going. That night I slept there and felt warm for the first time in my life. It was a wonderful discovery."

The rain fell heavily on the little hut. I could hear its heavy pitter-patter on the roof.

"I spent a lot of time in the forest. I ate berries, nuts, and roots, and even learned to cook them on the fire so they tasted better. But as the weather changed from fall to winter, food became scarce. I knew I had to leave the forest.

"I came upon a small cabin. It looked warm and dry. I really wanted to go inside. There was snow on the ground now and it was very cold. The door was open, so I walked in and saw an old man sat by the fire making his breakfast. He turned around as I entered and then screamed so loudly that it hurt my ears. He jumped up and ran to get away from me, just like you did after I took my very first breaths."

I could feel the monster looking at me, but I didn't look up. He continued his story. "I confess I ate the man's breakfast. It was wonderful. My stomach felt so full that I went to sleep right there on the floor.

"I knew I couldn't stay there after seeing the man's response to me. For the first time in my life, I walked into town during the day. People were shocked and scared. They screamed and ran away at the sight of me. Some even hit me with sticks and stones because they were so afraid. There was nothing I could do except run away and hide.

"What kind of a life is that, Frankenstein?" I shook my head in response, but didn't say anything.

"I ran from that place as fast as I could. I ran all the way out of town. I ran until I came to an old shack built next to a small cottage. Now, I knew not to go inside the cottage in case I scared the people and they tried to hurt me. I crawled inside the shack and hid there. It wasn't much, but I was safe.

"There was a small hole in the wall of the shack. I found that I could watch the family that lived in the cabin. I saw a young girl, whose name I soon learned was Agatha, carrying a pail of something into the house. Her brother met her at the door and took the pail from her so she wouldn't have to carry it any longer. The next time I saw the brother, whose name I learned was Felix, he was carrying some sort of tool and walking into the forest. When he returned, he had wood for their fire with him.

"I fell in love with that little family. They looked sad, but they were so hard-working. Their father was blind. He often sat by the fire playing a wooden flute. The music was so beautiful.

"I learned so much from them. I spent hours

and hours watching them. I learned to speak by listening to them. I learned to read by hearing them tell stories to one another. I watched as they were kind and good to their father. I felt this was how a family should be, and I wanted it for myself.

"They were very poor," the monster said, "but they were happy.

"I started to help them as much as I could. I stopped taking their food for my meals and went back to eating roots and berries. At night, I would borrow Felix's tools from the shed to chop piles and piles of wood for them. They were always so surprised to find a new pile on their doorstep in the morning!

"They lived a simple, quiet life. They were poor, but seemed content. I longed to talk to the sweet old man, to discuss Felix's books with him, to spend time helping Agatha in the garden. I wanted nothing more than to become a part of their family. I knew you didn't want me to be a part of yours, that you rejected me moments after you gave me life—but if I could find another place to belong, that would more than make up for the pain I felt after you left me.

"One day I was in the forest gathering food. I bent down to take a drink and saw myself in the water. Oh, I was a monster. A terrible, ugly monster. I hoped one day the family would look into my heart and see the real me, and not just look at my awful face.

"Almost a year passed. I decided that it was time now to try and meet this family I wanted so desperately to join. One morning I watched as Agatha and Felix left their father alone to take a walk in the woods. The old man picked up his guitar and played for a while. What beautiful music! It inspired me. I crawled out of my hiding place, walked up to the front door and knocked.

"I heard the old man call out for me to come inside.

"'Who are you?'" he asked.

"I told him that I was a traveler and asked him if I could warm myself by his fire. We sat and talked for a long time. I told the old man how I got there, how I had been living in the woods, and how I was a monster whom everyone hated. The man made all my dreams come true when he said I sounded like I had a pure, good heart.

"It was the moment of truth." Tears wet the monster's eyes. "Every inch of me wanted to tell him the whole story. So I did. I told him that it was me who cut the wood for them, who had helped them out for the past few months. The old man was shocked, but before he could say anything, his family returned to the cottage.

"Felix and Agatha were shocked to see me and immediately thought the worst. They cried out in fear and the boy dragged me away from his father. He threw me out of the house, and Agatha fainted. I knew I could have really hurt Felix, for I

was much bigger than he was, but I couldn't bring myself to harm him.

"I ran from there as fast as I could. My heart was broken in a million different pieces.

"I knew then I could never be a part of any family. I knew then that no one in the world would ever accept me because I looked this way. It didn't matter that I could read or write. It didn't matter that I could think or talk about philosophy or other great subjects. People would always be afraid of me. At that moment, I hated you, Frankenstein, for bringing me into a world that would never accept me."

CHAPTER 12

The Monster's Request

ﾟ⌒ﾟ

"I spent the rest of that night hiding in the woods. The next morning I went back to see if the little family was okay. When I got there, I heard someone say that they had left, fearing for their lives. Just seeing me for that short time made them think I would hurt them. They gave up everything they had just to get away from me. Imagine how it made me feel, Frankenstein.

"I never would have hurt them," he told me, "I loved them like they were my own family.

"I knew that I needed to find you. You alone

had brought me into this world and only you could give me a good life.

"My travels were long. It took me many months to get to Geneva." The monster looked out of the hut's tiny window at the rain falling outside. "I couldn't stop thinking about why you had made me if the whole world was just going to hate me.

"I lived in the woods just outside Geneva. Those were the same woods where I know you saw me that rainy night. One morning I saw William. He looked like such a nice boy. I thought that maybe someone so young could ignore my mean appearance. I watched him and his brother for a long time and heard them talking about you. For one short moment I thought I had found a member of my own family. This was the family that you brought me into and they would have to accept me.

"I watched as William hid from Ernest. He

stayed hidden until his brother gave up looking for him and left. That's when I came out of the bush. When William saw me, he screamed. I grabbed him so he wouldn't run away, but he wouldn't stop screaming. I held my hand over his mouth so he would be quiet. Soon, his limp body fell into my arms and I knew I had killed him. I saw the locket around his neck and took it. I left William there and ran away. I found the girl in the barn later that night and put the locket in her pocket.

"I knew it was wrong," he said. "I knew it was bad, but I couldn't help myself. I wanted to hurt you, Frankenstein, for giving me this awful, awful life."

Now, hours later, the monster finally told me what he wanted. "I can't spend any more time alone. You must make another being. You must create a friend for me, a wife—someone just like me. You are the only one who can do it."

The monster sat quietly after he finished his story. A lot of time passed as he waited for my answer. Finally I said, "No. I'm sorry, but the answer is no. I will never build another monster like you."

A light burned in the monster's eyes for a minute. We sat in silence. He tried to convince me that it was a good idea. "I am hated by everyone. I promise that I will leave forever if you do this one thing for me. If you do not agree, I will continue to hurt the people you love. You owe me, Frankenstein, do you not see that? All of this is your fault. You are the only person who can make it right."

"Do you really promise to leave forever if I build you a friend?" I asked. "And do you promise to leave my family alone?"

He replied, "I want you to build me a wife. Someone to spend my days with. Someone who is just like me. If you do that, I promise to leave forever. No further harm will come to you or your family, I promise."

I answered slowly. "Then I will do it, but you must know that I don't want to—but I will do it to protect my family."

"Thank you, Frankenstein," he said. "I will keep my word."

He looked at me carefully. "But know that I will be watching you. I will make sure you keep your promise to me."

He got up quickly and ran from the hut, leaving me behind. It took me many hours to find my way back to the mule. She was very hungry by the time I found her. We rode quickly back down the mountain. I spent the night at the inn, and woke up early the next morning after a poor night's sleep.

The long hike back to Bellerive was very hard. By the time I got home, it was the next day.

Having walked for so long without resting, I looked wild. My hair stood up all over my head and my clothes were wrinkled. At first, my family was shocked to see me that way, but then they were glad that I was home. Even though they wanted to know all about my trip, I couldn't tell anything that had happened over the past few days. I had a lot to think about, so I excused myself and went to bed.

CHAPTER 13

A Journey to England

༄

Days and weeks went by. I couldn't start the work. I knew this would make the monster mad. I had read about a scientist in England who was studying the female body. I knew his work would help me to create the monster's wife. I also knew it would also be a good way for me to go away for a while. I could explain to my father that I need to learn from this teacher—and it would give me time to create this new monster away from my family. I didn't want them to see me during this time.

I hoped, too, that it would keep the monster away from Elizabeth and my father. The last thing I wanted was for him to hurt the people I loved most in the world.

"Father," I said at breakfast one morning, "I would like to go to England. I've been feeling so much better lately. I think a trip would do me good. There's a scientist there whom I'd like to meet. He could help me with a project I'm starting."

My father smiled warmly at me. He looked happy and proud at that moment.

He said, "Well, Victor, I think that's a very good idea. But you must promise me something first. You know how much your mother wanted you and Elizabeth to get married. I'll give you permission to go to England, but only after you agree to get married when you get back."

I loved Elizabeth with all my heart and soul, but I was afraid. The monster had already killed my brother. What if he harmed her, too? I would never forgive myself if anything happened to her. I wanted to marry Elizabeth, but I had to solve my problems first. I couldn't tell my father about the monster. "Of course," I told him. "That's a wonderful idea."

He was so happy! We talked for a while longer about my trip. My father did not want me to go to England alone. He wrote to Henry and asked him to go with me. Everything was settled. Elizabeth was happy because she knew we would be married soon, my father was pleased that his family would soon be settled, and I was off to England.

Henry and I met in Strasbourg. We traveled across Europe and saw many wonderful sights. From castles to churches, from meadows to forests, the country between my homeland and England was amazing. But even Henry's good mood and the beautiful scenery could not make me enjoy myself. I had to start my terrible work again, and nothing could make me feel better.

It took us a full month to get to London. We traveled by coach, by foot, by boat—but finally, we arrived!

CHAPTER 14

On to Scotland

ᓚᥫᕤ

Once we arrived in the city, Henry quickly returned to his studies. He met with different language teachers and picked up where he had left off in Ingolstadt. We were back at school together, just like we were in Germany. I tried hard to hide my feelings. I didn't want him to see how unhappy I was to be studying science again.

Just seeing the laboratory brought back memories of the time when I made the first monster. How could I do it all over again? Thinking about the events of the past few weeks kept me awake night after night. What had I done? What had I promised?

Henry did well in his studies. He liked learning all he could about faraway places such as China and India. He wanted to enter into the trading business so he could visit the places he was learning about.

His good company kept the sad side of my work away. I was not the happiest man in the world, but at least I had a good friend by my side. In the end, Henry was happy enough for both of us. He met many new people and made lots of new friends. Often he would spend time out of our rooms visiting this person or that person. He always asked me to go with him, but I never did. The monster's request hung over me like a dark cloud.

I met regularly with the professor and learned a fair deal from his research. He gave me a lot of information about the female body and how it differed scientifically from the male. He was a kind and wise teacher. He taught me everything I needed to know to build the monster's wife. But still, it upset me to no end to know that everything I learned was for such a horrible project.

All of my time was devoted to gathering the tools I would need to work on the second creature. I had to make the monster's wife. The thought of making another creature made me sick, but I had promised and I could not go back on my word. I built a small laboratory. I had to be careful never to let Henry, or anyone else, see what I was doing. Just as I was about to start my work, Henry got a letter from Scotland. A good friend of his asked both of us to come for a visit.

I didn't want to go because it would mean putting off the work once again, but Henry insisted. I packed up my laboratory, careful to hide the proof of my latest project. I had so many trunks that we needed to hire a second carriage! Henry didn't mind. He was even more excited to see Scotland than he had been to visit England.

We traveled through lovely counties and sweet little towns. Almost a year had passed since the day I met the monster on the glacier of Montenvers, and I was no further ahead. But I had not seen or heard from the monster, so I tried to forget about him. I wanted to enjoy our trip.

A few weeks later, we arrived in the Highlands. After spending a month with his friend's family, Henry wanted to see more of Scotland. I knew I had to start my work. If I didn't do it now, I would never be brave enough to make the second creature. Henry noticed that my mood had been a little bit better since leaving London. He didn't want to go on alone and asked me to join him.

I said that I would be okay for a while by myself. He finally agreed, and decided to leave the next morning. I told him I would be fine. I would go to the Orkney Islands while he saw more of

Scotland. The islands were perfect for my work. There were almost no people there. I knew I would not be bothered while I finished my work. I didn't want anyone to see what I was doing. More importantly, I didn't want anyone to see the monster if he came looking for me.

The next morning, we both got ready to leave. Henry was still worried about me spending so much time by myself in such a lonely place.

"Henry, please don't worry! I'll be fine by myself," I said. "You need to go and have more fun. And I need to finish my project before I can go home to Elizabeth."

"Victor," he said to me, "I don't like it. But I'll go on by myself if you promise to meet me in Edinburgh in one month."

More promises! I didn't know if I'd be finished in a month, but now at least I had a reason to!

"Yes," I said. "That's a very good idea, Henry. I'll see you in exactly one month!"

With that we shook hands. Henry smiled and waved as he drove away in his carriage. It took me much longer to get everything packed up. Finally I was ready to leave, too. I was on my way to the Orkneys.

I rented a very rundown cottage in a tiny village near Kirkwall. It had three rooms. One of these worked well as a laboratory. Although I had everything I needed to start, I had to force my hands to do the work. It was that awful to me. A dark cloud fell over my mind during this time. I knew something bad was going to happen. I just didn't know what or when.

CHAPTER 15

The End of My Experiments

ᑫ

My time in the Orkneys was almost over. I was supposed to meet Henry in just one short week. It had rained almost the entire length of my stay. The gray skies were comforting, in a way. My mind was cleared by the cold, wet air. The work had come along, and I was almost finished.

Finally, it was time. The sun had set hours ago and I had worked late into the night. My room was dark because I had not lit any candles. "I'm finished!" I shouted out loud, "I've finished the second creature!"

The same sense of gloom that I felt after bringing the first creature to life returned. I stood and looked at her. The instruments of life were in my hands, but something stopped me.

The monster had agreed to leave, but this creature knew nothing of his plan. She didn't know she was for him. What if they didn't like each other? What if she didn't want to leave with him? What if she was even worse than he was? She would have a mind of her own. The monster could not control her actions any more than I could control his.

No, I thought to myself, *I cannot bring another one of these beings to life.*

I set down my instruments. I would not light the final spark. Suddenly, the monster appeared in the window! He saw me stop just before I finished. He watched as I put down the instruments and left the room. I shook my head back and forth to tell him it was over. I wouldn't be finishing this project. He saw me and groaned. His face fell and he started to cry. Seconds later, he burst into my cottage.

"Frankenstein! Why won't you finish the work?" he pleaded. "Why can't you bring her to life? You must keep your promise to me."

"I won't create another one like you," I said.

He insisted. "You owe me this much! I don't belong in this world. It is your fault that I am here. If you reject me as the rest of the world has done, I'll spend the rest of my miserable life unhappy and alone. Can't you see that?"

"I'm sorry," I said slowly. "But I will not finish this work. You could no more control this person than I could control you. You do not know what might happen if I bring her to life. I will not be responsible for any more creatures like you."

He looked angry and upset. "Please understand," I said. "I know you are unhappy, but this is not the answer. Now, you must go. I am leaving

this place tomorrow morning, and I am not taking my work with me. It will be buried on these islands forever."

The monster said coldly, "I will go, but I will never forgive you. You have broken your promise. You will pay for this, Frankenstein. You will. Your family is not safe. You are not safe. I will make you understand what it's like to be alone in a world where everyone hates you. Be warned. I will be with you on your wedding night."

He slammed the door behind him and ran away into the night. A cold chill went down my spine as I chased him outside. Before I could catch up, the monster had jumped into his boat and rowed away across the water. He was soon lost in the waves. I could no longer see him.

The cottage was quiet. The only sound I could hear was the ocean. His last words echoed in my ears. "I will be with you on your wedding night."

What did he mean?

"The monster must want to hurt Elizabeth!" I panicked. For the first time in months, I sat down and cried. I had to stop him at all costs. I had to stop him before he hurt everyone I loved in the world.

CHAPTER 16

The Accusation

∽

I woke up the next morning still angry with myself and with the monster. I left the cottage and spent the morning walking around like a ghost. I was far away from everything and everyone I loved. I sat on the beach for many hours that day. I was cold, wet, and hungry. Nothing could wake me from my walking sleep. Nothing, that is, except a visit from a man who brought me a stack of letters.

There were letters from my father and Elizabeth, but I was too sad to open these. There was also a letter from Henry. The sight of his familiar handwriting made me feel a bit better, and I opened the letter. It was full of funny stories about his trip. He told me about how much fun life was in Scotland. He also wrote about how well his plans to travel to India were coming together. He had gotten a letter from a friend in London, who wrote that he needed to get back there as soon as possible.

"Victor," he said in the letter, "I have to leave Scotland today. I know we were supposed to meet each other in Edinburgh, but why don't you travel to London instead?"

There was nothing keeping me in the Orkneys now. There was only the pain and regret of making so many mistakes. There was so much for me to do before I could go home. The first thing I had to do was clean up my last, unfinished experiment.

I started packing early the next morning. By

late afternoon, I had only one thing left to do. I had to pack up the laboratory. I gathered up all of my courage and opened the door. There were bits and pieces of my work spread out everywhere. This was the evidence of my broken promise.

First, I cleaned and put away my instruments. Then I took the poor creature outside. I said a quick prayer and buried her behind the cottage. The day had turned to night by the time I was finished. It would have been safer to wait until morning to cross the ocean in my boat. But my mind was made up to leave the island that very day, so that's what I did.

The dark sky was cloudy and I couldn't see the moon. There was little difference between the ocean and the sky. It was all black. The stars were hidden. For the second time in my life, I was afraid of the dark. I packed my things into the small sailboat and pushed off into the open water. The waves soon rose, and it was hard to sail. The wind blew strongly in the wrong direction. I found myself being carried out to sea. Several hours passed in this way. The more I tried to control the boat, the more it sailed off in the wrong direction.

As night turned into day, the wind calmed down. A gentle breeze now hit the sails. I was finally able to turn the boat back on the right course. The boat slowly found its way back to shore. I was happy to see a little town with a good harbor in the distance.

I was tying the boat up and taking down the sails when a crowd of people gathered around me. They whispered and pointed, making me uncomfortable.

"Hello," I said calmly, "would someone please tell me where I am? What's the name of this town?"

A man with a deep and threatening voice answered, "You will know soon enough! You may have landed somewhere you won't like. You will soon be shown where you'll be staying!"

I was very confused by his answer. It wasn't like strangers to be so rude.

"What's going on?" I asked.

"You are a criminal!" he replied. "We don't want you here."

"What are you talking about? Please, I've been out on the water all night, battling with bad winds. You must have me confused with someone else."

"We'll see about that!" he said gruffly. "You've got to go to see Mr. Kirwin, the judge. You can tell your story to him."

"Why do I need to see a judge? I haven't done anything wrong!" I said.

"As I said, tell it to him! There was a man found dead here last night. You are the only person we've seen come to town."

"Well, then, I'm happy to see your judge. I am totally innocent!" I said.

I followed the man away from my boat and

into town. The judge's office was in a lovely house in the center of the village. It didn't take long for us to get there, but the walk was hard. My stomach growled and my throat was dry. The long night on the water had made me tired. I wanted to lie down and go to sleep. With the crowd of angry people all around, I decided it was best to stay strong and to carry on.

Mr. Kirwin was a generous man with good manners. He called the room to order before asking, "Who brings this man before me? What has he done?"

The rough man who had brought me there answered, "I do, sir! We think he's the one who did it!"

The judge asked him to explain. The man said he had been out fishing yesterday with his brother and his son. On the way back from his boat, he had tripped over something. When he bent down to see what it was, he found a young man lying on the beach. They tried to wake him, but he was dead.

The man's brother spoke next. He had seen a man in a boat earlier in the day. He swore to the judge that it was the very boat that I sailed to shore. Next, a woman told the judge that she had seen this man push his boat back out to sea right where the poor boy was found. Several other people said that the winds must have brought me right back to shore as I tried to escape.

Mr. Kirwin decided that I needed to see the boy. He wanted to see my reaction, if I had any. Knowing I was innocent, I agreed. We walked to a room and he opened the door.

I saw my dear friend Henry Clerval lying there as cold as the sea I had crossed!

"No!" I wailed. "Henry, oh, Henry, not you, too! This is all my fault, my fault—"

My body could no longer take the pain and I fell to the floor. I spent the next two months in a fever. I was so sick that my life was often in danger. When I woke up, I found myself in jail. I had ranted and raved throughout my illness about how I had murdered my brother, put Justine in jail, and now killed Henry. I groaned loudly and woke up the nurse sitting beside my bed.

"Mr. Frankenstein! You're awake!" she said, sounding shocked.

I said quietly, "Yes. I hoped this was a bad dream. I'm sorry to be awake and in this awful place after everything that's happened. It would have been better if I had died."

"I must go and tell the judge!" She got up and left me alone in my cell. Mr. Kirwin came in shortly after she left. We had a long talk. The judge was both fair and polite to me. He had set up my care while I was in his prison, and had tried to make me more comfortable. He had gone through my things from the boat after I collapsed, and had seen the letters from Henry and my family. He knew I was educated and noble. He also knew I couldn't be guilty. But he couldn't set me free until I was proven innocent.

I thanked the judge for his kindness and asked quickly if he had had any word from my family. I needed to know if everyone was okay.

"Yes, they are fine. They are sad over the death of your best friend. They are also worried about your ill health. They know you are innocent. Now we just have to prove it to the rest of the court." He paused for a moment. "There's someone here to see you."

My first thought was that the monster was there, and I shouted, "No! I don't want to see him!"

The judge said harshly, "Young man, I should think the company of your father would be welcome to you under these circumstances. Why the outburst?"

"My father?" I exclaimed. "My father is here? Oh, yes! I would love to see him. I'm sorry, sir—I thought you were talking about someone else!"

Mr. Kirwin was surprised by the change in my tone. "I hope that's the last we see of your fever, young man," he said.

In a matter of seconds, my gentle father stood beside me. I stretched out my hand to him and said, "How are Elizabeth and Ernest?"

"They are fine, my son. I am sorry to see that you have had such an awful time. And poor Henry!"

"I am innocent, Father. You must know that."

"I know. I know." His voice was very soothing. "We've found someone from the Orkneys to speak at your hearing. He can say that you were on the island when they found our dear Henry. He handed you a package of letters when you were sitting on the beach!"

I had spent three months in prison by the time my case was heard. The jury believed my witness and they set me free. My father slapped me on the back. He couldn't hide his happiness. We walked outside and I took my first breath of free air.

"Father," I said, "we must go home right away."

He didn't think I was well enough to travel, but I insisted on leaving right away. We left early the next morning. We hired a ship that could take us directly to Geneva. I was very glad to be going back home. I sat on deck with my father and looked out over the sea. Henry was gone. Nothing could bring him back. My thoughts again turned back to the night I created the monster. My life had been destroyed by my work. Nothing could change that now. I quietly accepted my fate.

CHAPTER 17

The Return to Geneva

ᴄᴀ

Six weeks later, Elizabeth welcomed us both home with warm feelings and tears in her pretty blue eyes. I tried to be happy to see her, too, but the memories of the past few years overcame me. I didn't speak to anyone for days. Instead, I just stared out the window without moving.

My father sat down with me on the third day and said, "Please, dear son, we have had too much loss in our family. We must hold tightly to that which remains. We will have a small but happy circle. You must marry Elizabeth. Bring some joy into your life."

The words of the monster echoed in my head. *"I will be with you on your wedding night."*

"Father, I love her. You must believe that I do. But maybe it's not a wise idea for me to marry Elizabeth. I don't think I can make her happy. I am in such a terrible frame of mind."

"Nonsense. You love her and she loves you. That's the end of it."

The plans were made and our wedding date was set. Elizabeth's gentle nature often calmed my anger. We took long walks and learned to enjoy each other's company again. I was so nervous. I worried that something terrible might happen to her. I made a promise to myself. I would do everything in my power to make sure that no harm came to her.

Our wedding day was wonderful. My brother Ernest came home from the Foreign Service, and my father had never looked so proud. Elizabeth looked beautiful. I managed to act happy for her sake. Our honeymoon was set. We were taking a trip to Lake Como, in Italy. It was a special place for both of us.

While she packed our clothes, I took every measure to protect us both from the monster. Elizabeth didn't know that anything was wrong. I knew that I couldn't tell her. The story would simply scare her too much.

We left the morning after we got married. Those were the last moments of my life when I honestly felt happy. We enjoyed the beautiful scenery, and passed the wonderful Alps. We rode over stunning rivers, crossed thick green fields, and enjoyed the warm summer air.

CHAPTER 18

The Monster's Revenge

Night had begun to fall when we arrived at our inn. We took a short walk around Evian and ate our first meal as a family in our room. We were to travel to Italy first thing the next morning.

Suddenly, a rainstorm started. The water hit the windows with such power that we were both a bit frightened. As soon as it became dark, my calm, happy mood disappeared. After Elizabeth went to bed, a thousand fears rose in my mind. I was nervous and watchful. Every sound terrified me. But I didn't move. I stood guard with all the strength I could muster.

I walked up and down the hallways of the inn, searching for the monster. I looked in every corner, in every open room. There was no sign of him. For a moment I thought everything was going to be okay. Then I heard her scream.

I raced up the stairs and into our room. Elizabeth lay there on our bed. Oh, the monster had his revenge! My dear, sweet Elizabeth, who had never hurt a soul in her life, was gone. The monster had kept his word and given me a life like his own. I was doomed to spend the rest of my days miserable and alone, just like the horrible creature I had created.

I rushed to the open window to see if I could catch him. The air was cold and the rain blew inside the room. I saw the monster standing on the ground outside the window.

"Stop!" I shouted. "You villain! You killed my wife!" My shouting brought a crowd of people into my room. "That man just murdered my wife!" I yelled. "Quickly, we must try to catch him!"

The men raced outside with me while the women stayed behind to tend to Elizabeth's body. We tried to follow the monster's tracks, but it was no use. We couldn't find him. It was all too much for me and I fainted. The kind towns-people brought me back to the room and put me to bed. But I could not rest. Not when he was still out there. Not after he had ruined my only chance at happiness. I threw off the sheets and went into the next room to take a last look at my one true love.

"Oh, dear Elizabeth," I cried. "I am so sorry. I loved you so much, my darling." I took her in my arms and kissed her goodbye. The innkeeper and his wife were very kind to me. They said they would make sure Elizabeth arrived back home safely. I wrote my father a quick letter. I told him that I was going to find the man who caused all our heartache.

I rushed out into the night to find the monster. I didn't know where he went or where he was going, but that didn't matter. The only thing that mattered was finding him.

I knew I would never go home again. This thought made me very sad. I knew my father would be very unhappy, too. But I didn't want to cause him any more pain. He and Ernest would find it hard enough to go on after the death of Elizabeth. The only honor in my actions would be to finish what I had started.

I raced out of the inn. I could hear an echo far off in the distance. It was coming from the lake itself. It was a loud and evil laugh.

"That's him!" I cried. "He's on the lake."

I jumped into a boat and started to row with

all of my strength. Thus, the long journey began. I've chased him for many months now. From the shores of Switzerland to the cold, icy fields of Russia, he ran and I ran after him.

My life was miserable. There were no comforts of home, no friends to cheer me up, and no family to love. But I knew I would not find peace until I found and destroyed him.

When I reached St. Petersburg, the monster had left me a note: "You are still alive, Frankenstein. But I know you are unhappy. Follow me now to the icy kingdom of the Arctic. You will feel the misery of the cold and the frost. If you want to catch me, you must do as I say."

I would never give up the search. I started off for the Arctic in my sled. The dogs drove north. The cold was almost too much to bear. He left me clues along the way, short notes that I was going in the right direction. The colder it got, the harder

I pushed. The only thing driving me forward was the thought of finally meeting the monster and ending everything for good.

The dogs were very fast. They allowed me to catch up to him as I had never been able to before. I came into a small village and asked the people there if they had seen anything.

One man told me that he had seen a terribly ugly man drive through on his own sled hours before I arrived. The monster had stolen some food and taken off after scaring most of the people in town. To the horror of these men and women, he took off in the direction of no man's land.

"No one can survive out there," he said to me. "He will either be frozen to death or be stuck on the ice floes. Either way, he will never be seen again."

I thanked him for his information, and then

bought some supplies for the long journey ahead. The land thundered underneath me. The ice cracked and water leaked through. The cold bit at my nose, my ears, my fingers, and my toes. But I didn't stop. And then at last, I saw him! He was just a mile in front of me, so I pressed on.

The wind rose and the sea roared. With a mighty shock like an earthquake, the ice split wide open. I was stuck on a piece of the floe. All hope of ever catching the monster was gone, and I floated out to sea. I would certainly not survive the night trapped on one small piece of ice.

Hour after hour went by. The ice slowly melted underneath me. I almost gave up all hope. My life would end in this frozen, barren land. I would be unable to finish what I had started.

CHAPTER 19

The Last Days of Victor Frankenstein

"That's when I saw your ship, Captain Walton," he said. "I had to act fast, so I broke my sled into oars and rowed my way toward you. I had decided that if you were going to sail south that I would carry on to the north. I didn't want the monster to get away."

"Well, it's a good thing you came on board," I said to him. "We saved your life, my friend."

"Yes, and I thank you kindly for that. But I need you to promise me that you'll find the monster if I don't make it, that you'll bring him to justice for everything that he's done, for everything I've gone through."

I promised to do just that. Then Frankenstein collapsed, worn out, on the bed, and fell into a deep, troubled sleep.

A week passed. I wanted to make him feel better, to ease his troubled mind, but I knew I couldn't. Frankenstein's health was very poor. We stayed inside and talked the days away.

"When I was younger," he said to me one morning, "I believed I was meant for greatness. The feelings were so important to me that I didn't think of anything else. I gave up my entire life for science, for that one goal of creating life from nothing."

He paused and wiped the tears from his eyes. "And I lost everything."

I worried that Frankenstein's health would finally fail and he would be taken from me. After wishing for a good friend for so long, I didn't want to lose him. We spent so much time together that I couldn't imagine my life without him. But I knew he had greater concerns.

"I will chase him until the very end," he said. "That is the only way for it to be over."

The mountains of ice threatened to crush our ship every minute of every day. My crew was scared. Even I was afraid we wouldn't make it back to England. I felt I had let them down. These men had trusted me with their lives. It would be my fault if we didn't make it back. My selfish need to see the land no other man had seen would be the end of so many lives.

Frankenstein comforted me as I worried. He tried to tell me the ice would break up and that we would see the blue skies of England once again. I found it hard to believe him, especially as I looked at the worried faces of my men day after day.

Finally, a few sailors came to see me in my cabin. They told me the crew no longer wanted to go on. Even if the ice opened up, they wanted to turn the ship around and sail for home. They wanted to see their families. Could I blame them?

So I told them that yes, we would turn around when the ice opened up and freed the ship.

The very next morning there were shouts of joy all around as we heard the loud sounds of the ice cracking and breaking up. When I went for my daily visit to see Frankenstein, he asked me what the commotion was all about. He could hear the cheers from the deck. I told him that the ice had moved and we would sail for home as soon as we could free the ship.

"No!" he said quickly. "I can't leave this place until I find the monster. I have to leave your ship. I won't go back with you."

He tried to get up, but it was too much for him in his weakened state. He fell over and fainted on the bed. I called for the ship's doctor, who came right away.

"I'm afraid he's very sick," the doctor said to me as Frankenstein rested. "He'll be lucky if he makes it through the night."

"Thank you, doctor," I said. Then I returned to Frankenstein's bedside. I would keep him company in those last hours.

We talked more about his life and about what had happened. He told me it was the right decision to turn the ship around. "The lives of these men," he said, "are more important than our own selfish goals."

He continued, "That's a lesson you should be very aware of, my friend. Take comfort that I learned it for you and pay close attention to my mistakes." He pressed my hand firmly and then closed his eyes forever, a gentle smile passing over his lips.

The tears flowed from my eyes. I wiped them away quickly and walked out of his cabin for some fresh air. I had only been on deck for a couple of seconds when I heard a strange noise coming from Frankenstein's room. I rushed down there and found the monster standing beside the bed!

He was huge. Much bigger than any man I had ever seen before. His face was hidden behind long strands of hair and his large hand sat on Frankenstein's shoulder. He heard me open the door and turned. When he saw me standing there, he jumped toward the window.

Oh! That face! It was the most horrible thing I had ever seen in my life. I shut my eyes without thinking, but then called out for the monster to stay.

"Wait!" I said.

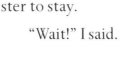

He stopped for a minute, and then said to me, "This is all my fault! I've done this to him. I took away everything he loved and now my creator is gone!

Oh, Frankenstein, I am so sorry. I am so sorry for everything that happened."

The monster cried out in pain. "Farewell, Frankenstein, farewell! You can believe me now. I will keep my word. I will leave the world of men forever. I will no longer see the sun or the stars. I will no longer cause your family any pain. Oh, dear creator—I know you can't forgive me, but at least now you can rest."

With those words, the monster leaped from the cabin window. I ran to it as he jumped out and onto an ice floe. The waves soon took him away, and I lost sight of him in the darkness and distance. It was finally over, just as Frankenstein wanted. I would remember him, the monster, and their terrible story for as long as I lived. And just as he wished, I took Frankenstein's mistakes to heart. I turned my ship around and headed for home.

What Do *You* Think?
Questions for Discussion

‿∽

Have you ever been around a toddler who keeps asking the question "Why?" Does your teacher call on you in class with questions from your homework? Do your parents ask you questions about your day at the dinner table? We are always surrounded by questions that need a specific response. But is it possible to have a question with no right answer?

The following questions are about the book you just read. But this is not a quiz! They are designed to help you look at the people, places, and events in the story from different angles.

These questions do not have specific answers. Instead, they might make you think of the story in a completely new way.

Think carefully about each question and enjoy discovering more about this classic story.

1. This book is told from the perspective of three different characters. Why do you think the author chose to do that? Have you read any other books that are narrated in a similar manner?

2. Captain Walton says, "I had a crew of great men on board my ship, but they took orders from me. They were not my companions." How do you think this made the captain feel? Have you ever felt this way?

3. Frankenstein says to Captain Walton, "I want to tell you the whole story. I think it may help you find your own way." What do you think this means? Do you think that hearing about other people's experiences can help you solve your own problems?

4. The two people whom Frankenstein cares for the most, Elizabeth and Henry, are very different people. Which of these are you more like? Do you know anyone who is like either of these characters?

5. After leaving his professor's lab, Frankenstein says, "What a wonderful day it was… it decided my destiny." Do you believe a single day can decide the course of someone's life? What event in your life has affected you the most?

6. Do you think the fact that William's locket showed up in Justine's pocket was enough proof to convict her? How was her trial different from trials today?

7. The monster asks Frankenstein why he was created if the whole world was just going to hate him. Do you think Frankenstein gave much thought to his creation's feelings when he was creating him?

8. How is the way in which the monster learns about the world different from the way in which Frankenstein grew up?

9. On his way to the Orkney Islands, Frankenstein says, "I just knew something bad was going to happen. I just didn't know what or when." Have you ever had a similar feeling? What happened?

10. Frankenstein and Captain Walton each say that his passion has led to disastrous results. Do you think passion is a good thing or a bad thing? What are you passionate about?

Afterword

❦

First impressions are important.

Whether we are meeting new people, going to new places, or picking up a book unknown to us, first impressions count for a lot. They can lead to warm, lasting memories or can make us shy away from any future encounters.

Can you recall your own first impressions and earliest memories of reading the classics?

Do you remember wading through pages and pages of text to prepare for an exam? Or were you the child who hid under the blanket to read with a flashlight, joining forces with Robin Hood to save Maid Marian? Do you remember only how long it took you to read a lengthy novel such as *Little Women*? Or did you become best friends with the March sisters?

Even for a gifted young reader, getting through long chapters with dense language can easily become overwhelming and can obscure the richness of the story and its characters. Reading an abridged, newly crafted version of a classic novel can be the gentle introduction a child needs to explore the characters and story line without the frustration of difficult vocabulary and complex themes.

Reading an abridged version of a classic novel gives the young reader a sense of independence and the satisfaction of finishing a "grown-up" book. And when a child is engaged with and inspired by a classic story, the tone is set for further exploration of the story's themes, characters, history, and details. As a child's reading skills advance, the desire to tackle the original, unabridged version of the story will naturally emerge.

If made accessible to young readers, these stories can become invaluable tools for understanding themselves in the context of their families and social environments. This is why the *Classic Starts* series includes questions that stimulate discussion regarding the impact and social relevance of the characters and stories today. These questions can foster lively conversations between children and their parents or teachers. When we look at the issues, values, and standards of past times in terms of how we live now, we can appreciate literature's classic tales in a very personal and engaging way.

Share your love of reading the classics with a young child, and introduce an imaginary world real enough to last a lifetime.

Dr. Arthur Pober, Ed.D.

Dr. Arthur Pober has spent more than twenty years in the fields of early-childhood and gifted education. He is the former principal of one of the world's oldest laboratory schools for gifted youngsters, Hunter College Elementary School, and former Director of Magnet Schools for the Gifted and Talented for more than 25,000 youngsters in New York City.

Dr. Pober is a recognized authority in the areas of media and child protection and is currently the U.S. representative to the European Institute for the Media and European Advertising Standards Alliance.

Explore these wonderful stories in our
Classic Starts library.

20,000 Leagues Under the Sea

The Adventures of Huckleberry Finn

The Adventures of Robin Hood

The Adventures of Sherlock Holmes

The Adventures of Tom Sawyer

Anne of Green Gables

Black Beauty

Call of the Wild

Frankenstein

Gulliver's Travels

A Little Princess

Little Women

Oliver Twist

The Red Badge of Courage

Robinson Crusoe

The Secret Garden

The Story of King Arthur and His Knights

The Strange Case of Dr. Jekyll and Mr. Hyde

Treasure Island

White Fang